WHEN SANTA WAS LATE

Written by
Frank R. Leet

Illustrated by
Buford Austin Winfrey

IDEALS CHILDREN'S BOOKS
Nashville, Tennessee

ATTENTION: SCHOOLS AND CORPORATIONS
This book is available at quantity discount with bulk purchases for educational,
fund-raising, business, or premium use. For information, please write to:
Special Sales Department
P. O. Box 140300
Nashville, TN 37214

ISBN 0-8249-8483-8

Every effort has been made to locate the copyright holder of this poem.
The publisher apologizes for any inadvertent copyright transgression.

In memory of my mother, Estelle Austin-Winfrey,
who inspired me to study fine art.

- B.A.W.

'Twas all because a youngster
Had the measles, so they say,
And rashly wrote to Santa Claus
One cold December day.

Old Santa always fumigates
His Christmas mail, I know.
I don't see how a measle germ
Could have the slightest show.

But germs are mighty stubborn things—
Of course, not easily seen;
So Santa, all bespeckled now,
Was soon in quarantine.

The North Wind brought the tidings
While blustering to and fro
In countless daily journeys
Through the lands of ice and snow.

And when the news was told about,
Storekeepers everywhere
Shook their heads, threw up their hands,
And groaned in great despair.

For days were speeding swiftly
And Christmas drawing nigh,
"Can Santa do his shopping?"
Became their daily cry.

Christmas morn arrived at last,
And with it such a wail
From out a billion childish throats,
That Santa Claus should fail

To fill each tiny woolen sock
With knickknacks as of yore,
And cover every Christmas tree
With shining things galore.

The Old Year heard the sobbing
And the wailing through the land,
And, seeking old King Winter,
Quite secretly they planned.

The Old Year spoke, "Your Majesty,
'Twould be a dreadful thing
For any self-respecting Year
No Christmas joys to bring!"

"Quite so, indeed!" King Winter quoth,
"You've been the best of Years.
'Twould surely be regrettable
To disappoint the dears.

I'll call a mammoth meeting
Of all the People of the Snow;
Someone among these loyal folks
Will have a plan, I know."

And thus it was, Snow Landers
In sparkling gay array
Forgathered in the palace hall
Just at the break of day.

Now there was old King Winter
With locks and beard of snow;
Jack Frost, the jolly beggar boy,
Came with the Queen of Ice, you know.

And North Wind came, of course,
'Twas hard to keep him quiet.
He tumbled all the elves about
And almost caused a riot.

When order was restored at last
The king made known his will.
Said he, "Beloved Snow Folks all,
You know good Santa's ill.

"And Christmas almost five
    days late!
'Tis surely plain that we
Must carry out the good Saint's job
Tonight, from A to Z."

So every head was bowed in thought—
Tho' odd to say, the crowd
Was not so very quiet, since
They each one thought out loud.

At last the Queen of Ice arose
And raised a jeweled hand.
"Why not," said she, "send Snow
 Elves out
All up and down the land,

To go from town to town
And visit all the stores
And buy the gifts for boys and girls
To leave at all their doors?"

"It shall be done, Your Majesty!"
The faithful Snow Elves cried,
And whisking off on ice cycles
Went speeding far and wide.

They stopped at every store to fill
Their sacks with splendid toys,
And then were off to visit homes
Of sleeping girls and boys.

Next morn old Santa woke and heard
All o'er the white clad earth
The melody of Christmas chimes
And childish cries of mirth.

While on his sill wee Snow Elves sat
And squeaked to his delight,
"A Merry Christmas, Santa Claus!
We did it in the night!"